THE GOWN

A SHORT STORY

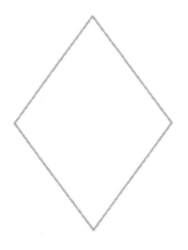

EMILIE AUTUMN

The Gown / Emilie Autumn
ISBN 9780998990941

Contents

The Gown

"Oh, no, dear," said the nurse, "the ties go in the back."

"The back?" said the girl. "Really? Are you sure?"

The girl's chest was bared, her stomach showing plain through the two sets of string ties that held the gown loosely together, and yet, for all the absurdity of it, this present humiliation was more comprehensible to her than the equal exposure of her backside. Such vulnerability was unthinkable.

By the time the doctor entered the examining room six minutes and twenty-three seconds later, the girl had put the gown right. She had taken her place on the examining table as a means to hide her near nakedness prior to his arrival. The thin, waxy paper covering the table stuck to the backs of her thighs, crinkling loudly as she attempted to pull the gown more snugly behind her, and she thought how much it was like the paper that the meat was weighed out on and wrapped up inside of at the butcher counter her mother shopped at on Sundays when the chicken was half price because it was four days old.

It was to be only a routine examination, just a check-up, followed by the influenza vaccination that every twelve-year-old was required to undergo prior to the start of the school term. She had been to the doctor before, of course, but she had always been allowed to keep her own clothes on. Once, when she was three, they'd taken off her jumper to check her heartbeat (she remembered this quite clearly—the jumper had been blue), but that was all.

She had never been ordered to put on the gown until today, and, as soon as she held the thin cloth in her hands, white, and patterned all over with pale blue diamond shapes, everything in the little room seemed different. The examination table looked longer and somehow challenging, like an empty stage. When she hopped up and sat upon the edge, it felt harder than she remembered, despite the thin padding beneath the paper. The tools arranged so neatly upon the steel tray set squarely on the countertop looked sharp and heavy, and she knew that, if she touched them, they would be cold. The fluorescent lights above her head flickered in an irritating way she had never noticed before, and they emitted a faint buzzing sound that confused her mind and hurt the very insides of her ears.

When the doctor glanced at her, his eyes did not look kind as she was sure they had when she was smaller. As he approached her, she felt shy—painfully shy—for the first time in her life.

"Back to school?" asked the doctor, as he lifted his stethoscope to his ears.

Without waiting for an answer, the doctor told her to take a deep breath in. The metal was ice upon her back, breaking her out into goose flesh. She felt embarrassed by her reaction—ashamed of her lack of control over her own skin. She hoped the doctor hadn't noticed. In agony she breathed three more times and felt the tears pricking at the insides of her eyelids.

The doctor then moved around to her front where he hit her on the knee with his rubber mallet and made her kick—a silly, stupid kick. "What on earth is this for?" she wondered. What could the doctor possibly tell about her from this ridiculous little kick? She wanted to ask, but felt sure that, if she spoke, her voice would come out all jittery—that she would give away how cold she was, how painfully cold was the air now upon her exposed back—and she didn't want the doctor to know how uncomfortable she felt. Besides, it didn't really matter what the rubber mallet proved, did it? It wouldn't change anything about her life if she knew.

The doctor seemed to be satisfied with her eyes, her ears, her nose, and now he took a syringe from a paper wrapper and told her to make a fist with her left hand. Looking down at her arm, she saw why he had told her this, for her veins, pale and blue and twisting, shown more vividly to the surface as she began to clench her hand. She curled her fingers into her palm, pressed her thumb across them tightly, and tried to feel strong. She imagined having to fight someone who approached her from behind, who saw her exposed as she was, and, as she felt the fear creep up and over her bare shoulders where her gown was slipping away, she squeezed her fist harder still.

Before she knew that it had gone in, the needle was being drawn out, and the doctor was reaching to his steel tray for a cotton pad. As his back was turned, a single drop of blood fell from her arm to the gown below, just above her left knee. She looked up quickly to see if the doctor had noticed. He had not. As he swiveled round to her and moved to tape the cotton pad over the punctured skin, she covered the blood spot with her right hand.

The doctor rose and walked to the door.

"You can go ahead and get dressed now," he said, without looking at her. "You're all set until next year."

She looked down to where her hand still covered the spot on the gown. She prayed to God that, when she removed her hand, the spot would be gone. But it was still there. She felt panic then, and hurried to the little sink and ran the cold water, only a weak stream so that no one would hear. Cold water for blood, she had once heard someone say—she could not remember who. Cold water for blood. Who in her life would have said that? She lifted the hem of the gown to the sink. Her backside was completely exposed now, and she looked at the door to see if there was a lock. There was. But if she locked the door and someone were to try and come in . . . She couldn't lock the door. She would simply have to hurry. "Cold water for blood," she thought. "This must get it out. It must!"

As the stream of water hit the thin material, the spot only grew in size, as if she were still bleeding onto the fabric. She felt her heartbeat quicken. She rubbed the spot with her fingers faster and faster until it faded slightly, but it would not be made gone, and now it was even larger. Where the spot had first begun eight pale blue diamonds away from the side seam of the gown and thirteen diamonds up from the hem, now it was only four diamonds from the side seam and nine-and-a-half from the hem.

She had meant only to wet the bit of gown that carried the spot, but, as she turned off the faucet and wrung out the fabric, she felt her face go hot all over, for the wetness had spread, and the whole lower half of the gown was soaked. Her arms felt suddenly weak, the gown hanging heavy about her legs now, making her knees wet and cold. She must hide it. She must hide this horrible thing—this hideous thing—this shameful thing.

She pulled it off over her head without undoing the ties and her pulse pounded in her ears as she looked frantically around the little room for a place to hide the gown, but there was nowhere that wouldn't be found right away, and she needed time—time for other patients to come in and out of the room so that, when the gown was finally found, it might be said to have belonged to anyone.

Then, she heard footsteps in the hall. She turned back to the examination table, to the thin padding that covered it, and, before she could think better of it, she crumpled the gown into the smallest bundle she could and stuffed it beneath the padding. "Oh, how stupid!" she thought. "That was the wrong thing! I ought to have thrown it in the trash!" But the footsteps were nearly at the door and it was too late. She rushed to pull on her dress just in time for the knob to turn.

For two months after the appointment, her heart leapt every time the phone rang. She would freeze every muscle, every nerve in her body, as her mother answered the call. She imagined what the person on the other end of the line was saying—trying to discern, through the first few words uttered on her mother's part, who the caller might be. When her mother gave a rare little laugh within the first five or six seconds of the call, she knew she was alright—at least this time. But when there was a period of awful silence after the first "*Hello?*"... well, then her body ran cold, she felt the chill upon her back, and she thought, "Cold water for blood, cold water for blood, cold water for blood..." until her mother said something that identified the caller as being someone safe. Then she could breathe, though she was still dizzy for the rest of the day, and had nightmares.

Whenever she woke in a sweat, she would try and think sensibly. "The crackling paper," she would tell herself. "They change the paper every time—not the padding. They might never change the padding but once a year because of that paper."

She had hated the butcher paper against her thighs; hated how the sound it made showed the doctor that she was embarrassed—that she was trying to cover herself from him. But now she was grateful for the paper, for they could change it five hundred times and might not find the ruined gown for a year. Then, she would recall the doctor's parting words to her. "You're all set until next year," he had said. And she knew that she could never go back there. She could die of influenza, but she could never go back.

It was seven years later that her stomach began to hurt—a dull, burning pain just below her rib cage. "Is this appendicitis?" she wondered. No, it couldn't be appendicitis. Appendicitis was the lower abdomen and to the right, she read, and this pain was higher up and in the middle.

At first, her stomach only hurt after she ate. Then, it hurt all the time and she couldn't sleep. One night, it hurt so badly that she could scarcely draw breath, and she called a taxi to take her to an emergency room because she knew that they would be open all night. She didn't know how she would pay, but they couldn't turn her out, she thought, surely they couldn't, and she was working now. She would find a way.

In the back of the taxi, she almost cried, and this frightened her because she never cried. She bent over and held her knees so that the driver wouldn't see her eyes sparkling in the rear-view mirror. It was bad enough that he was taking her to the hospital in the middle of the night. What must he think of her?

When she was in the lobby at last, she said to the woman at the front desk, "I feel like I'm burning. Like I'm being burned alive from the inside out."

She was told to sit down and wait. The chairs were dirty and the room swarmed with sound, but there was nothing she could do and so she closed her eyes. Still she could hear the children screaming close around her, the children who had an ear infection, or the children of tired mothers who were ill themselves, and she thought, "I never screamed like that—not for any reason."

After two hours and fourteen minutes, the woman at the front desk called her name and she tried to rise from her chair, but she doubled over and it took a nurse to lift her and lead her, wobbling like a newborn calf, to the small examining room.

"There's a gown on the bed," said the nurse, before bustling away and down the hall.

She could barely lift her blouse over her head, and she was glad that she had worn a skirt that could just drop to the floor instead of jeans or something with loads of buttons. When she finally had her arms through the sleeves of the gown, she couldn't find the strength to do up the ties behind her; the pain had numbed her arms through to the fingertips. She could only hold the sides of the gown together behind her back as she struggled up to the bed, raising her left knee over the edge. Then she stopped. Upon the gown, just above her knee, was a small red spot.

Trembling in every limb, she lowered her foot and lifted the fabric to inspect it more closely—the fabric that was thin and white, with pale blue diamond shapes, faded in some areas, but very much visible. The spot was faded too, more of a rust color than a true red, as though it had been washed several times. "A coincidence," she thought. "A harmless coincidence." And then . . . but no, she wouldn't do it. She absolutely would not count. Well, perhaps she *would* count, but only from the bottom—from the hem. One, two, three, four, five . . . nine-and-a-half diamonds from the hem. *Nine-and-a-half.* But from the side seam . . . she would not count them. Not for a million dollars would she count the diamonds from the side seam. But this was all too silly. She was a grownup now, and on her own, and must not be silly anymore. Certainly she ought to count the diamonds as quickly as possible, for then she would know that it was not the same gown at all, because of course it wasn't. If she didn't count, she would always wonder. And so she counted. And once she had finished, she began to cry in earnest.

Another wave of burning nausea had overtaken her, and there was no way she could climb up to the bed now. They would have to lift her up, and they would see the spot. No, she couldn't let them find her like this. The shame, she decided, was more horrible than the pain, and so she clawed her way up to the bed at last, and she lay there, and she waited.

After sixteen minutes and four seconds, a doctor entered the room. She had forgotten to cover the spot, and she thought to do so now but was petrified by the idea that her sudden movement might draw attention to the spot, and so she remained still and hoped.

The doctor did not see it, for he simply came to her side and placed his hands on her stomach and pressed hard and moved them around and pressed again before saying, in a strangely satisfied manner, "You have an ulcer."

"What does that mean?" she asked him. "Don't only old men get ulcers?"

"That's actually a misnomer," said the doctor. "Anyone can get an ulcer, under certain conditions, though I will say that it is rare for someone your age."

"What conditions?" she asked.

"Well, some common reasons are dietary, because it's got to do with an over-production of acid that burns away the lining of your stomach, eventually making a hole in that lining, and this can lead to internal bleeding, which is what we need to check for in your case."

"You said 'reasons' . . . what are the other reasons?" she asked, as he wrote down some words on a chart.

"Oh, yes . . . stress. Stress can actually cause the body to over-produce acid in a similar way to what a bad diet will do. What is your living situation?"

He did not look at her as he asked this but continued to make his notes so that she couldn't be certain he was listening, and she couldn't quite describe her living situation anyway, so she only said, "I'm stressed, I think."

"And why is that?" asked the doctor, who had apparently been listening after all.

But she couldn't think of how to begin. There was no beginning to her story—no door by which to enter the room where it all slept and screamed and raged depending upon the day or the hour—and so she gave up and simply said, "Things have happened to me that should not have happened."

The doctor had finished his notes and was preparing an IV drip now. He suspected that her stomach had begun to bleed inside, or that's what she thought he'd said, but she couldn't really be sure because she couldn't hear anything anymore except for the buzzing coming from the fluorescent lights overhead.

"I'm angry," she said. "I'm angry all the time."

"Anger is a form of stress," said the doctor, and she was surprised to find that he could hear her over the buzzing of the lights. "Have you tried talking to a therapist?"

"I can't afford that," she said, and the doctor left the room.

She looked at the IV needle embedded in her left arm and the vision reminded her of the gown and the spot and how it had all begun. Glancing through the doorway into the hall to make sure that no one was coming, she quickly lifted her right arm to the back of her head and felt for a hairpin. She pulled one loose, and then, while she still had the strength, she put the tip of one of the pin ends into her mouth and bit off the little plastic bulb that coated the sharp metal. She spat the plastic to the ground, then took up the bit of the gown that bore the spot. She placed the sharp end of the pin directly over the center of the spot and held the fabric as taut as she could with her left hand, all the while trying not to tear the IV needle loose from her vein. Finally, she pressed the pin until it came through the other side of the spot with a violent pop. "There," she thought. "Now you have an ulcer too."

She had absolutely no way of knowing. She had swallowed only one tiny pink pill each morning, just as prescribed, nothing more. She wasn't feeling ill. She wasn't feeling different at all, in fact, which did disappoint her slightly. But, upon disembarking from the plane, there it had been—the voicemail message from her psychiatric doctor, speaking in an impatient tone he had never used towards her during the three years they had been meeting. The results of her blood tests were in, he said, and she was to please call him on his personal line at whatever hour she received his message.

As she walked through the terminal, she dialed the number of the doctor's personal line, already feeling guilty that the hour was so late, at 10:37 P.M. The phone rang, and she realized that she had never spoken to her doctor past late afternoon. Was she allowed into his world once it was dark out? "Will he even remember my name at this hour?" she wondered. Surely he left her at the office, along with all of his other patients. Surely he did not take her home with him—not to his family, not to his dinner table, not to his private thoughts.

On the fourth ring, the doctor answered.

"Where are you?" he said, without asking who it was. "I left you a message hours ago."

Was he angry with her? Had he any right to be?

"I was on a plane," she said. "I'm in New York. I told you I was moving here. Being in Los Angeles was a mistake for me—I told you that. Anyway, I only just landed. I'm sorry."

"You left?" he said, and now he was angry—she was sure of it. "You left before your blood test results were in?"

Why was he asking? Hadn't she just told him she'd left?

"I didn't know I wasn't supposed to. You never said—"

"You should never leave a state only a week after starting a new medication," said the doctor, as though she had been deliberately bad and had indeed known better. "Listen, you're in the airport still? Alright. I need you to go into a shop and buy the largest bottle of water you can find, and then drink it all as quickly as you can. After that, you need to get to a hospital. Tonight. As soon as possible. Any emergency room should be able to handle this."

"Handle what?" she asked. "What's wrong with me?"

"Your blood is showing a toxic level of lithium, and this can cause permanent neurological damage, among other things," he told her. "You're going to need kidney dialysis, in all likelihood. An emergency room can usually perform—"

"Toxic? What does that even mean? I only took the amount you told me to," she said.

"Honestly," he said, "it doesn't make any sense to me either, but test results don't lie. Are you drinking the water? Have you been feeling dizzy or nauseous, or experiencing muscle aches? Have you been feeling uncoordinated, or having trouble speaking?"

"I'm drinking the water now. What is 'trouble speaking'? I always have trouble speaking."

"Like slurred speech. Are you slurring your speech?"

"I don't think I'm slurring."

"You should be feeling horrible," the doctor said.

She pulled her two blue suitcases from the carousel, searching for the exit nearest the taxi stand, and wondering if she had been slurring her speech without realizing it. *Her* speech, the doctor had said. But was it really hers? Could speech belong to any one person? She spotted the blue diamond-shaped sign painted with the symbol of a car and rushed towards it. As she ran, she began to feel uncoordinated.

Once in the taxi, she had to ask the driver which emergency room was nearest and could they please go there directly, and she wondered if she was slurring, but he didn't seem concerned either way and lurched away from the curb and the blue diamond.

When they reached the emergency room twenty-seven minutes and fifty-three seconds later, the driver helped to lift her luggage from the trunk, and she tipped him far too much, and then she hurried again and felt dizzy. Trailing her two large suitcases behind her, one in each hand, she sailed past the sliding glass doors and into the lobby where she was nearly deafened by the buzzing of the all-too-familiar fluorescent lights.

She explained her doctor's message to the guard at the front desk. It was now nearing midnight. Was something happening inside her? Was she slurring her speech? Was she going to die? Was it possible her test results had been mixed up with someone else's? How was kidney dialysis done?

She was in a hospital gown now. She noted the speed at which the gown was always produced—the gown seeming a prerequisite to even the most perfunctory conversation between doctor and patient, as though a medical person were morbidly uncomfortable speaking to an invalid in plain clothes—as though the clothes made the patient somehow indecent and the gown was modest and proper and made the medical person very comfortable.

Without the gown, no man of great knowledge and skill would so much as ask her name, but by the time she was in the gown these men always had her chart, and so they didn't need to. The gown had become a staple of her wardrobe, a reviled relative that would not die and kept visiting even though he was not wanted and he knew it very well.

When she had seen the thin white fabric draped over the back of the chair inside the small, curtained area she had been led into, the fabric patterned with pale blue diamonds, the buzzing of the lights grew louder still and she was afraid she might fall. But the nurse had stood by her as she changed, and she was relieved to look down to the area above her left knee and see that there was nothing notable about the fabric besides a general wearing away of the pattern here and there.

Surely it was not strange that every hospital, every doctor's office she had ever remembered visiting since she was twelve-years-old, had offered her a gown of this same fabric. Variety was not demanded, and there would naturally be only one resource from which all of the medical centers across the country obtained their necessaries. What mattered was that there was no spot. No spot at all.

"I'll have your suitcases taken to our storage area," said the nurse, turning to go. "It might get a bit crowded in here once the machines are brought in."

And then, she paused and looked mortified.

"Oh, my goodness! I am so sorry, honey, that gown is dirty—it was from the last patient and it hasn't been cleaned. Let's get that off right away. You can cover yourself with this blanket."

The nurse pulled the crisp sheet from the bed and traded it for the dirty gown.

"I'll be right back with a fresh one."

The girl who was not a girl anymore but a young woman was quite sure that she did not slur her speech as she thanked the nurse and raised her head to look up at the lights flickering in the ceiling, the buzzing fluorescent lights.

The curtain opened with a scrape and a rattle and another folded gown was placed upon the bed.

"Go on and change into that one," said the nurse, "and the doctor will be here in just a few minutes."

As she dropped the sheet and unfolded the gown, she tried to prepare herself for what was to come, without knowing what was meant to happen to her at all. They had called her doctor and spoken to him about the test results, and that was all that mattered to anyone; she was merely the ignorant keeper of the body under discussion. She had left the state and tried to go somewhere else, somewhere she liked, where she knew a few people, where she could work and do what she was meant to do, and here she was, back at the hospital again, wearing this faded white gown that left her exposed in the back, patterned with those goddamned pale blue diamonds, and then her eyes passed over the fabric above her left knee and she stifled a scream.

As she lay in the bed, with needles in her arm and tubes connecting her to the machines that were taking out her blood and cleansing it, she pressed the fabric between her fingers and wondered why. The spot was nine-and-a-half diamonds from the hem, four diamonds from the left side seam—she had counted thirty-three times—and it was as clear and red as ever, though the gown itself had surely been washed a thousand times or more, covered the shivering shoulders of a thousand sick women, and still been found fit to remain in service. The hole in the center of the spot was the pupil of the eye that could see directly into the back of her mind, the eye that followed her wherever she went, no matter how far she traveled, and watched her always. It was the eye of the darkness she had imagined when she had made the fist—when she had felt the cold creep over her shoulders and she had broken out in goose flesh and she had prayed that the doctor wouldn't see. But the eye saw.

It was early morning before the machine was finished with her. The tubes were removed, and, as she was helped down from the bed, the cold air hit her back like the slap of an open hand. Her fingers were raw where she had rubbed the stained fabric of the gown between them for the past five hours and twenty-nine minutes, and it was with significant difficulty that she untied the two knots that just barely kept the gown from falling off altogether.

As she struggled, she became angrier and angrier. Why were there only two ties? Why didn't it close all the way down the back? Why? And so, as soon as she was alone, she twined the strings around her fingers and called upon what remaining strength she had and pulled as hard as she could.

Afterwards, she crumpled up the gown and stuffed it into the rubbish bin. As she hurriedly covered it with a layer of tissues, she saw the spot with the hole in the center staring up at her accusingly, and no matter how many tissues she threw in the bin, she could still see it.

In the taxi on the way to her friend's apartment—the apartment that was currently empty and had been allowed her the use of for two weeks while she got acquainted with her new city and found a place of her own—she reached inside her pocket and drew out four strings of fabric. Each string was eight inches long and only a quarter of an inch wide, but still she could see the faint outlines of the pale blue diamonds, and, as she pulled the strings across her palm, she saw the frayed ends where they had been torn, and she smiled.

"Are you going to die?" he shouted into her face, and she couldn't tell whether he was afraid that she would say yes or whether he was hoping she would.

Her psychiatric doctor had convinced her to come back from New York so that they could continue treatment—so that they could find the right pill, he had said, or combination of pills, as the lithium clearly had not been the answer. Everyone was different, he had told her, and she had to be patient. "I am patient, you are doctor" she had replied, and he had not laughed.

She hadn't wanted to come back, but she couldn't find a new doctor that would accept her insurance, and she couldn't pay the full price, and so she had to return. Being without medication was not an option, and so she was reeled again into the cold black pit where the darkness was waiting still—waiting for her back to be bared to it once more.

Over the two years since her return, she had been given a multitude of different medications, sometimes several pills together—"cocktails", as her doctor called them—but nothing seemed to be working, and she knew now that it was never going to let her go. It had never any intention of letting her go. And so she took everything she could find at the bottom of her handbag until she fell asleep, and it all seemed so justified—it seemed that she was doing only what she had always been meant to do—that is was surprising to hear the anger in the voice of the man who found her. He didn't even like her very much—she knew this. Why couldn't he simply be glad for her? Why must he shout at her this way? She was just so tired.

"Are you going to die?" he shouted again, shaking her violently by the shoulders.

"I don't think so," she said with a deep sigh—the resignation of a desperate failure.

She had entered the hospital by the same emergency entrance, but she was taken to the top of the building now, where people roamed the halls, the dirty white gowns patterned with pale blue diamonds falling from their bony frames, their lank hair smelling foul. No one had any shoes, and no one looked anyone in the eye.

She was not allowed to put on the gown herself this time. She was not allowed to undress in privacy. She would not need privacy anymore. As she stood naked, her arms held out agreeably before her, the warden slipped the gown—the faded cloth of shame and degradation—up and over her shoulders and left the room.

"At least I have been allowed to tie myself," she thought. That one thing she had been allowed to do. She was not beaten yet. She was not dead. But when she reached for the back of the gown, when she felt the edges of the opening, she found that there were no ties at all. She tore the gown from her body and held it to her face—brought the spot with the hole in the center right up to her face—and she laughed. She laughed until the warden came back, and when two more men in uniforms came towards her with tethers in their hands, she was still laughing.

The walls were padded, and there was only the light from the tiny window high up in the door to see by. But there was nothing to see anyhow, not anymore. The darkness was close behind her all the time now, and she realized that it always had been. How foolish she had been to run away. How foolish she had been to make a fist. But even as she thought this, the fingers of her left hand folded into her palm, and her thumb closed over them, and she squeezed tightly until she became dizzy and fell into the waking sleep that was all she ever had now—the sleep that held no dreams.

The cell door was opened, and the eyes of the student nurse blinked quickly as they adjusted to the darkness. It took all of ten-and-a-half seconds before he could make out the figure of the young woman lying upon the floor, her left hand clenched into a fist that looked as though it strained her whole body even as she slept.

As the student nurse approached the young woman, he could see that her lips were moving, but the words were so faint that they could not be distinguished. The nurse bent down to the body on the ground and drew in his breath.

"How could they be so unfeeling, making a young woman wear a gown without any ties at all," he thought. "She's completely exposed, and, good heavens, it's got blood on it too, and a hole . . . this is awful. I should tell someone to get her something new. A little dignity might even help her. But it's only my first day at this hospital, and I mustn't say anything—I mustn't cause any disturbance—not yet. Maybe someday."

The young woman on the floor suddenly clutched the hem of her ragged, stained gown and rubbed it between her hands in a frantic motion. As she did so, the words she had been muttering grew louder and the nurse leaned closer to see if he could make them out.

"Cold water for blood," said the young woman, "cold water for blood, cold water for blood, cold water for blood . . ."

At least this is what the nurse thought she said, but he couldn't be sure because her speech was slurred.

Other Works

by

Emilie Autumn

NOVELS:

The Asylum for Wayward Victorian Girls

MUSIC ALBUMS:

Fight Like A Girl
Opheliac
Laced/Unlaced

Many more writings, albums, and other works
available at www.emilieautumn.com.

Study Guide

for

The Gown

1. How did you feel as you read the story? Confused, sad, anxious, amused? How did your feelings change as the story went on?

2. Have you ever been made extremely uncomfortable, or even frightened, by something that seemed harmless to everyone around you?

3. How do you feel about the main character? Did you like her, identify with her, find her annoying, even dislike her?

4. What three words would you use to best describe this story?

5. Did the story make you remember events in your own life, and reconsider them in any way?

6. Was there anything in the story that you could strongly relate to?

7. Describe the main character. What were her personality traits, motivations, inner qualities?

8. Why do you think the main character behaved the way she did? Why do you think she was so uncomfortable wearing the gown? Why was she frightened?

9. What main ideas does the author explore in The Gown? Are there any particular themes that stood out to you?

10. What do you think the author's purpose was in writing this story? Does the writing style make you think the story is autobiographical or entirely fiction?

11. Who do you think is narrating the story? Do you think it is an unknown witness? The author herself? The main character?

12. Why do you think the main character is so afraid for people to see the blood spot? What do you think she believes would happen if they saw?

13. Do you believe there was ever any blood spot at all?

14. What do you think happens to the girl after the story is over? What do you think happens to the student nurse?

15. Do you think it is important that the story takes place in a medical environment, or do you think the story could have taken place anywhere?

16. Describe the relationships between the main character and the various doctors and nurses in the story. Do you think the medical people are trying to help her? Hurt her? Or are they just doing their jobs?

17. If the main character, the girl, is the protagonist of the story, who is the antagonist? The gown? The spot? The darkness? The doctors?

18. Do you think that this same story could have taken place with a boy as the main character instead of a girl? Why or why not?

19. Do you believe that there was an actual dark entity that was trying to trap the girl, or was this all in her head?

20. Why do you think the passage of time is counted so meticulously throughout the story? Who do you think is counting? The narrator, or the girl? If it is the girl who is counting, then why are we told that "ten-and-a-half-seconds" pass even after she is asleep in the padded cell?

21. Was the ending of the story satisfying? If you could re-write the ending, what would you have the characters do?

22. If you could continue the story in another chapter after the ending, what would you write?

23. Do you think the main character was mentally unstable from the very beginning? Do you think she is mentally ill by the end?

24. Does the main character remind you of yourself, or of anyone you know?

25. Do you think anything occurred in the main character's life prior to her first doctor visit that prompted her to react to the gown in the way she did?

26. Have you had an experience as a child that haunts your life even now that you are older? If so, what was it? How are you affected by it today?

27. What do you think the main character's life is like during the years between her appearances in the story? She claims to have a job at one point. What do you think this job is? When she says that she can do what she is meant to do in New York, what do you think she is meant to do?

28. When the main character tells the doctor that things have happened to her that should not have happened, what do you think she means?

29. What do you think the main character looks like?

30. What do you think the main character's childhood home life is like? Why is she alone most of the time? Does she have a father? Siblings? What is her relationship with her mother like?

31. How does the main character change from the beginning to the end of the story? Does she undergo any transformations or does she stay the same? Do you think she has learned anything, about the world or about herself?

32. Do you think there is any significance to the number of years that go by between the reoccurrence of the gown?

33. Do you think the narrator is telling you the truth about what is happening to the main character? Do you believe what you are being told?

34. Do you believe that the blood spots are really in the gowns that the main character is told to wear? If so, how do you think it is possible that the gown is the same one from the first scene? If not, how do you think the student nurse can see the blood spot at the end of the story?

35. Has this story changed you in any way? Is there anything or anyone that you think about differently now that you have read it?

36. If you had to pick a favorite quote from the story, what would it be and why?

37. Why do you think the main character has so many medical problems that require her to go to a hospital?

38. Why do you think that none of the psychiatric medications that the main character was given had worked for her? What do you think her problem actually is?

39. What do you think was the significance of the buzzing fluorescent lights? Why were they so loud? Do you believe anyone else heard them?

40. If you could meet the main character for tea, what would you say to her?

41. If you could have tea with any of the medical people in the story, what would you say to them?

42. If you were given the gown right now and told to put it on, would you do it?

43. Do you think the author is criticizing anything in our culture or society, or do you think she was simply telling a story for entertainment?

44. Do you think it is a good thing for children to be very sensitive? What are some benefits and drawbacks of being a sensitive person in general?

45. Do you think that adults are capable of understanding the experiences of children and how they perceive the world, or have we changed too much since our own childhoods?

46. If you were casting the movie version of this story, who would you cast as the main character? As the doctors and nurses?

47. Have you read any of the author's other works, and, if so, did you find any significant similarities or differences between The Gown and these other works? Do the author's works tie together in some way?

48. If you could ask the author a question about the story, what would you ask?

49. The next time you see your doctor and have to wear a gown, will you be looking for a blood spot above your left knee?

50. Have you ever had an ulcer? They suck.

Made in the USA
Middletown, DE
22 February 2018